This book belongs to

....

Quarto is the authority on a wide range of topics.

Quarto educates, entertains and enriches the lives of our readers—enthusiasts and lovers of hands-on living.

www.quartoknows.com

© 2018 Quarto Publishing plc

First published in 2018 by QED Publishing, an imprint of The Quarto Group.
The Old Brewery, 6 Blundell Street,
London N7 9BH, United Kingdom.
T (0)20 7700 6700 F (0)20 7700 8066
www.QuartoKnows.com

A catalogue record for this book is available from the British Library.

ISBN 978-1-78493-922-9

Based on the original story by Emma Barnes and Hannah Wood
Author of adapted text: Katie Woolley
Series Editor: Joyce Bentley
Series Designer: Sarah Peden

Manufactured in Dongguan, China TL102017

9 8 7 6 5 4 3 2 1

MIX
Paper from responsible sources
FSC® C104723
www.fsc.org

Reading
Gems

Where is the Cat?

Ted, Bess and Dad were on the farm.

Ted and Bess looked in the barn.

It's not in here.

Ted and Bess looked in the house.

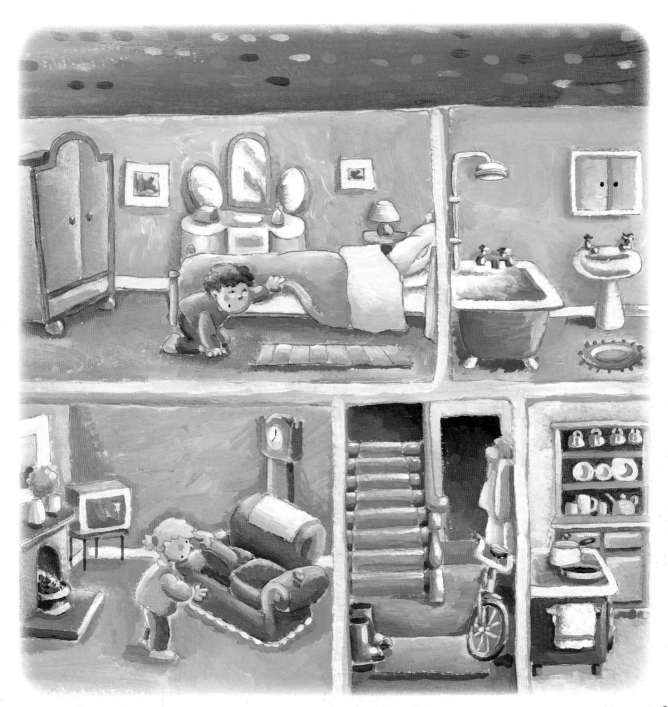

Ted and Bess looked
in the field.

The cat is
not here.

The cat was not with the hens.

The cat was not
with the goat.

The cat and the hat
were not on the farm.

Is the cat in the barn?

Story Words

barn

Bess

cat

Dad

farm

field

goat

hat

hen

house

Mum

Ted

Let's Talk About
Where is the Cat?

**Look carefully at
the book cover.**

What objects and animals
can you see?

What other things might
you see on a farm?

What noises
might you hear?

**Have a look at the family
on pages 20 and 22.**

How do you think the
family are feeling?

How can you tell?

What other things can you
see on page 22–23?

Look at picture on page 22–23.

Why did the cat go missing?

The cat has Dad's hat. What other objects does it have in its bed?

What is your favourite animal?

Can you draw it and write its name underneath the picture?

Talk about the end of the story.

Did you like the ending?

What do you think the characters did next?

Fun and Games

Read the sentences aloud and
find a picture to match.

It is a cow.

It is a duck.

It is a hen.

It is a goat.

Can you match these sentences to the correct character in the story?

Where is my hat?

Here is the cat!

Miaow! Miaow!

The cat is not here.

Your Turn

Now that you have read the story,
have a go at telling it in your own words.
Use the pictures below to help you.

GET TO KNOW READING GEMS

Reading Gems is a series of books that has been written for children who are learning to read. The books have been created in consultation with a literacy specialist.

The books fit into four levels, with each level getting more challenging as a child's confidence and reading ability grows. The simple text and fun illustrations provide gradual, structured practice of reading. Most importantly, these books are good stories that are fun to read!

Level 1 is for children who are taking their first steps into reading. Story themes and subjects are familiar to young children, and there is lots of repetition to build reading confidence.

Level 2 is for children who have taken their first reading steps and are becoming readers. Story themes are still familiar but sentences are a bit longer, as children begin to tackle more challenging vocabulary.

Level 3 is for children who are developing as readers. Stories and subjects are varied, and more descriptive words are introduced.

Level 4 is for readers who are rapidly growing in reading confidence and independence. There is less repetition on the page, broader themes are explored and plot lines straddle multiple pages.

Where is the Cat? is all about things going missing on the farm. It explores themes of family, life on a farm and animals.

Level 1